10 Minutes Fairy Tales

The Jungle Book

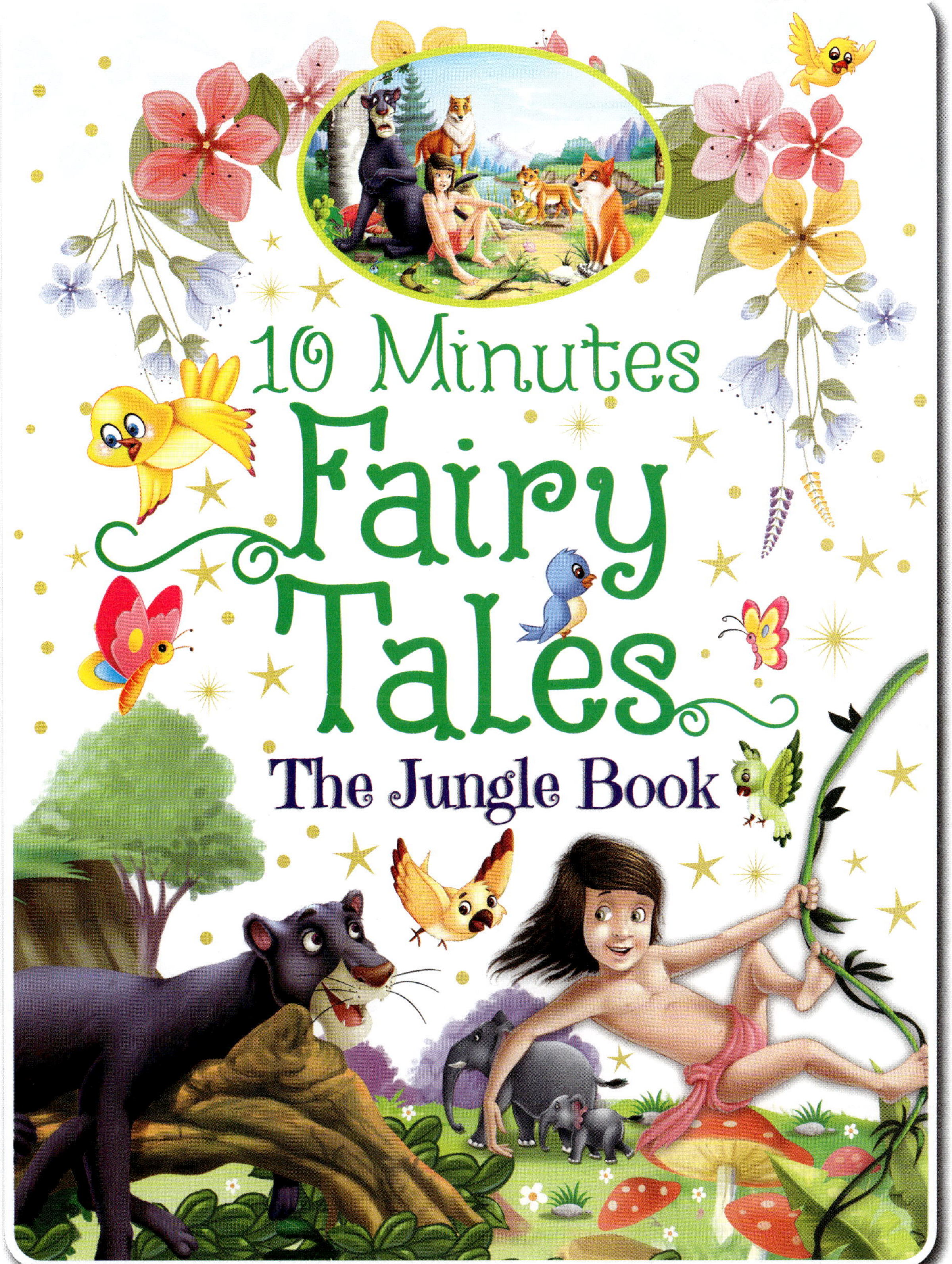

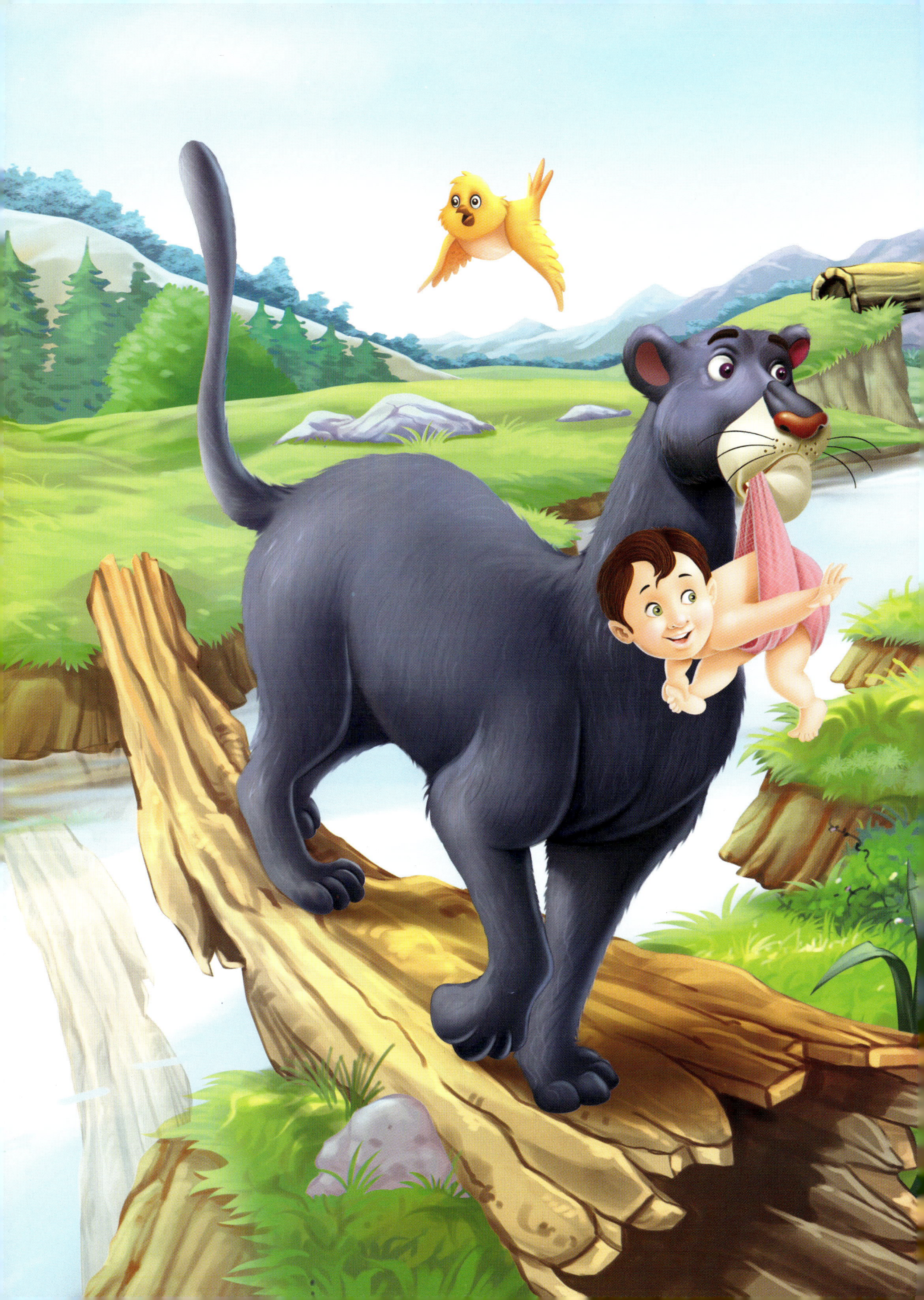

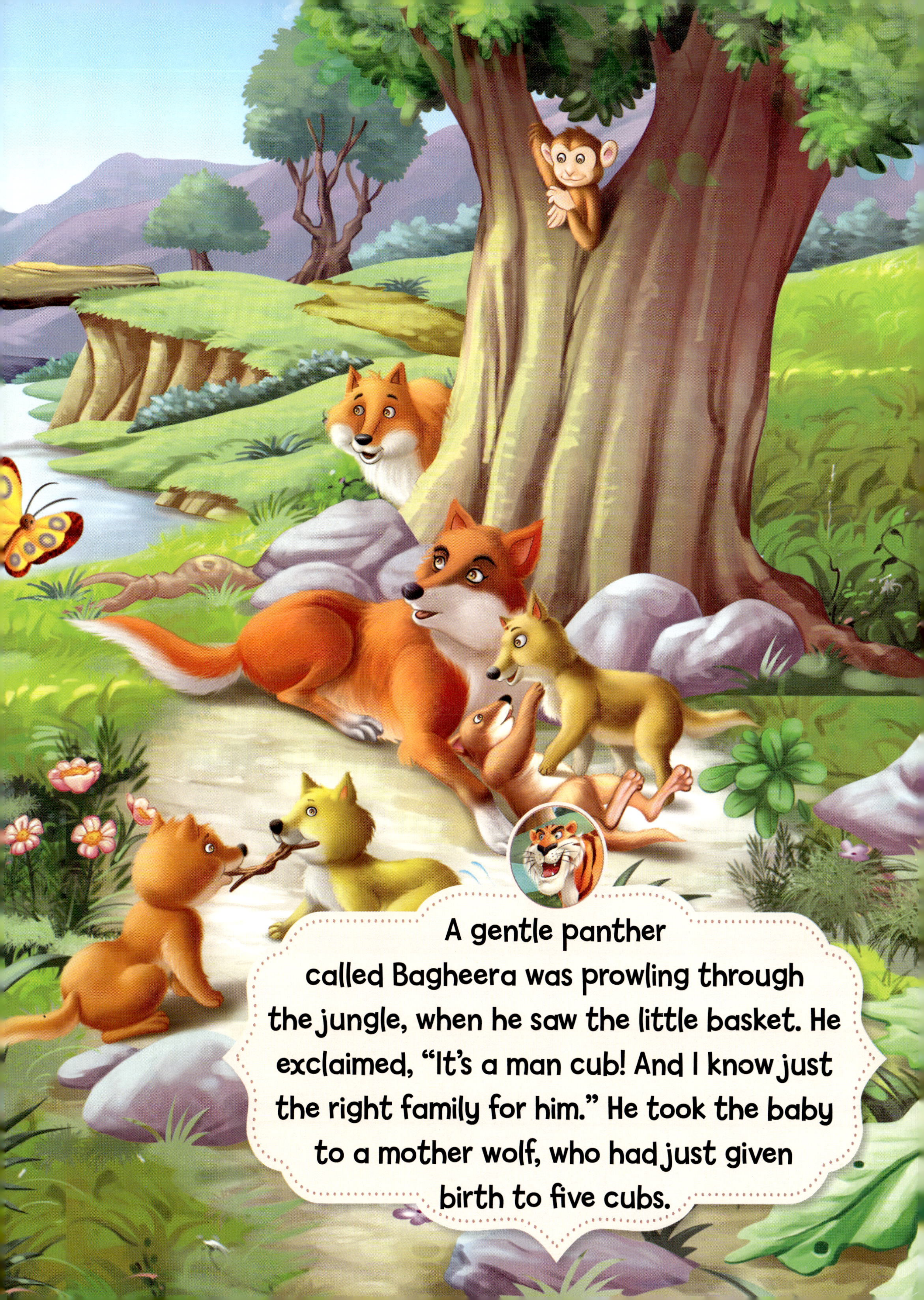

A gentle panther called Bagheera was prowling through the jungle, when he saw the little basket. He exclaimed, "It's a man cub! And I know just the right family for him." He took the baby to a mother wolf, who had just given birth to five cubs.

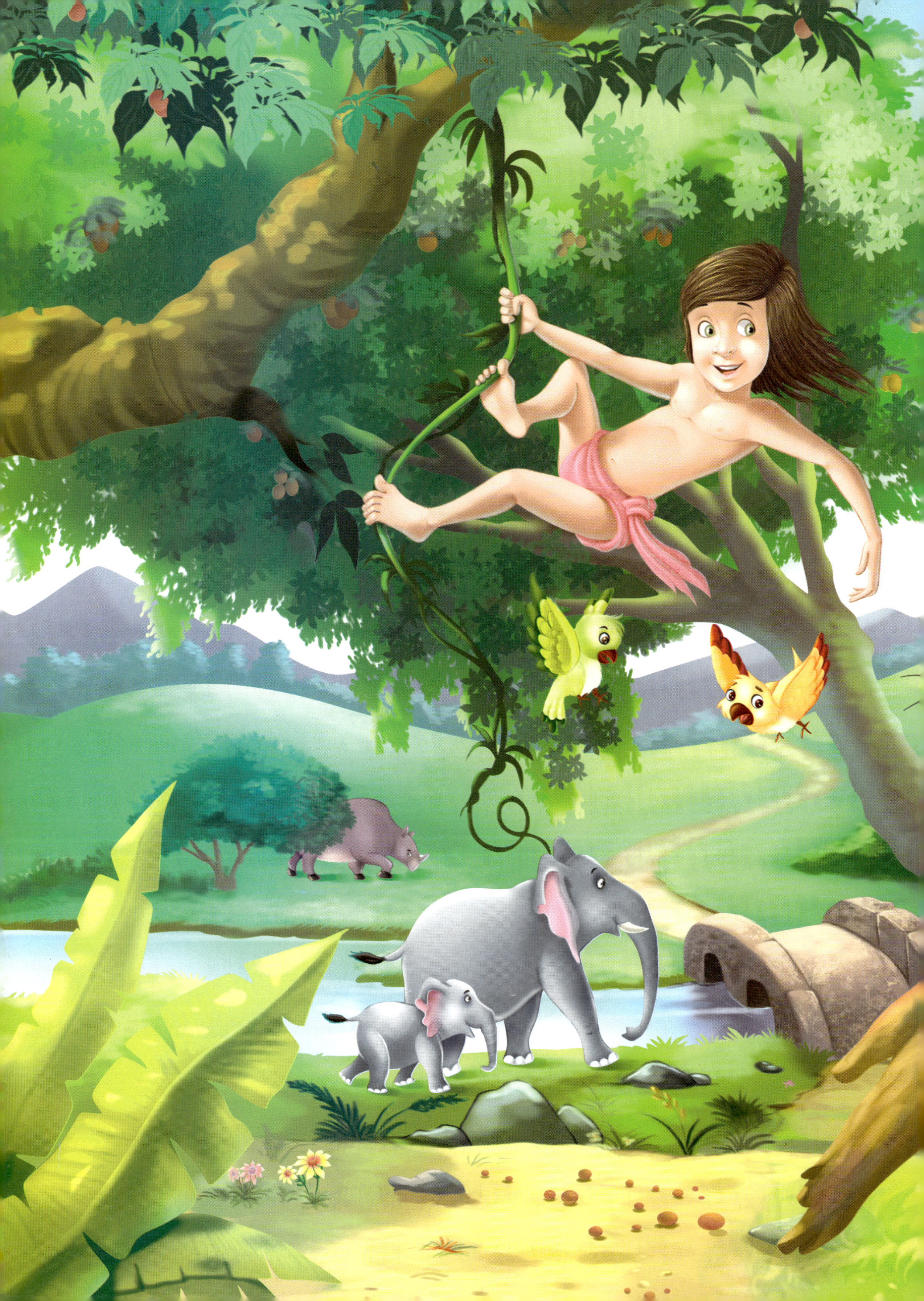

The mother wolf raised the baby boy happily along with her own cubs. He began growing up in the jungle. The man cub was named Mowgli. Mowgli soon became familiar with the life, ways and laws of the jungle. He loved his best friend, Bagheera, and the wolves.

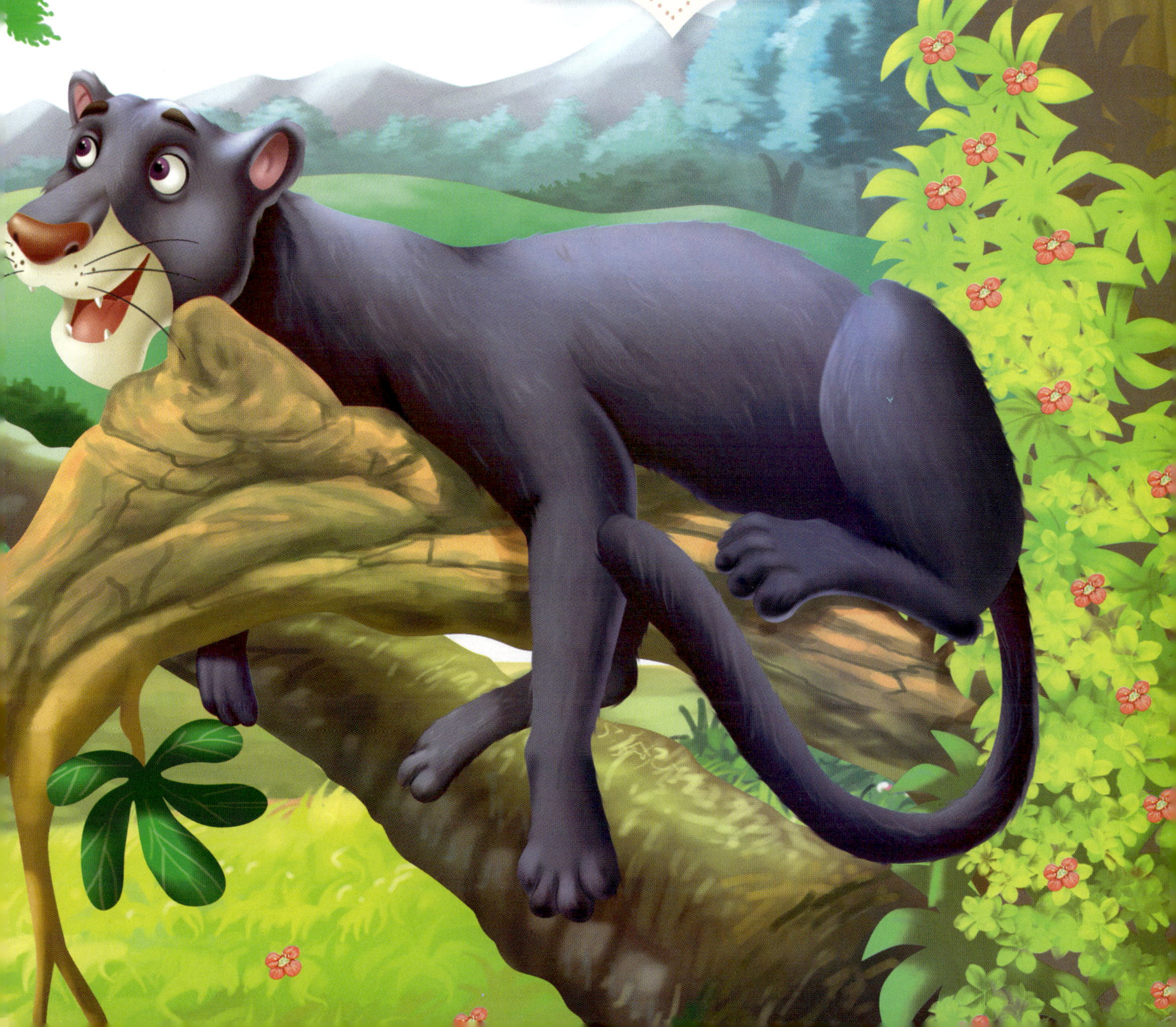

One day, Shere Khan, a
man-eating tiger, was returning to his den after a kill. He often went into the village and killed men, turning them against the rest of the jungle dwellers. Soon news reached Shere Khan ears that there was a man cub in the jungle. He wanted to find and eat the man cub as quickly as possible.

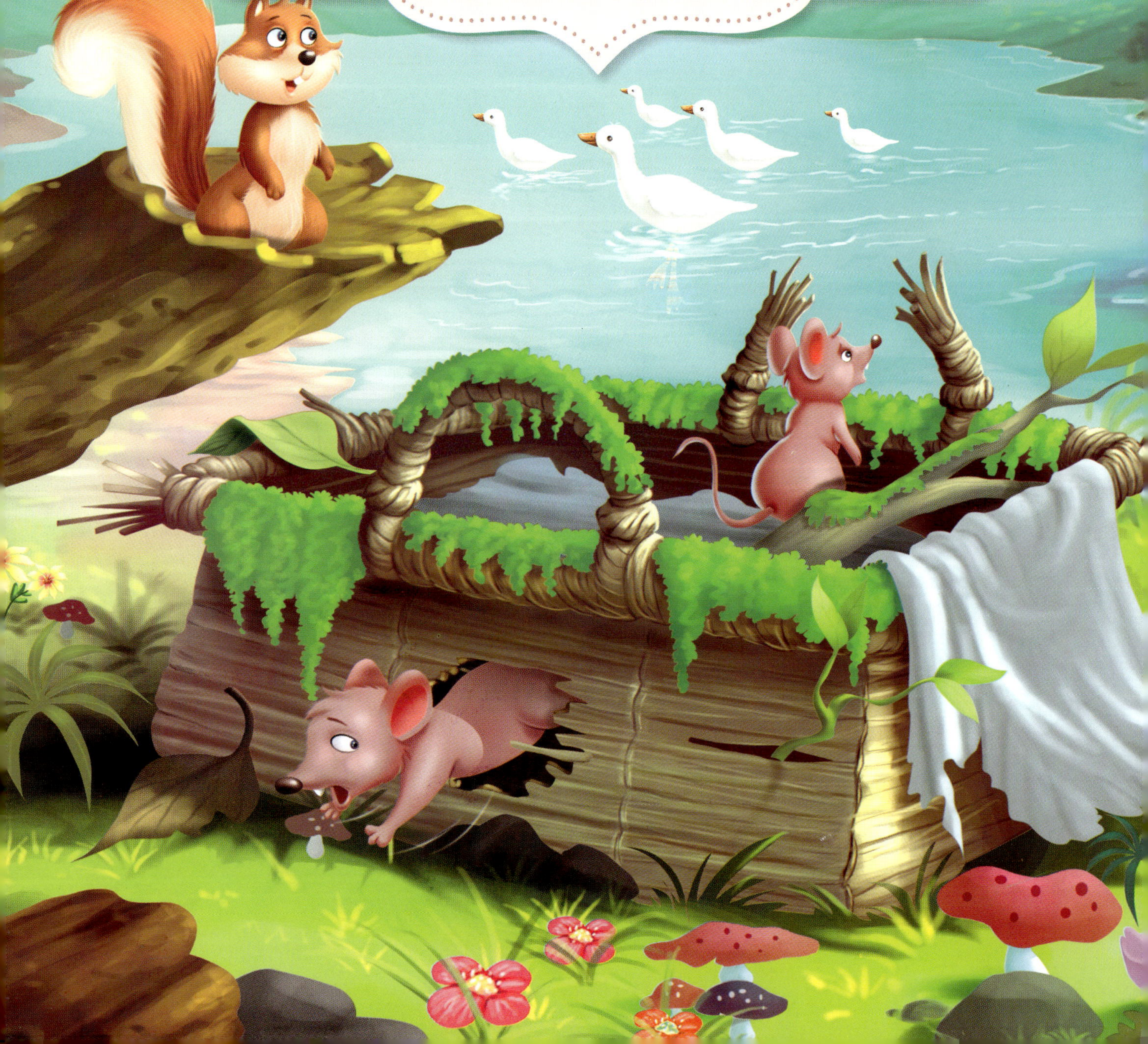

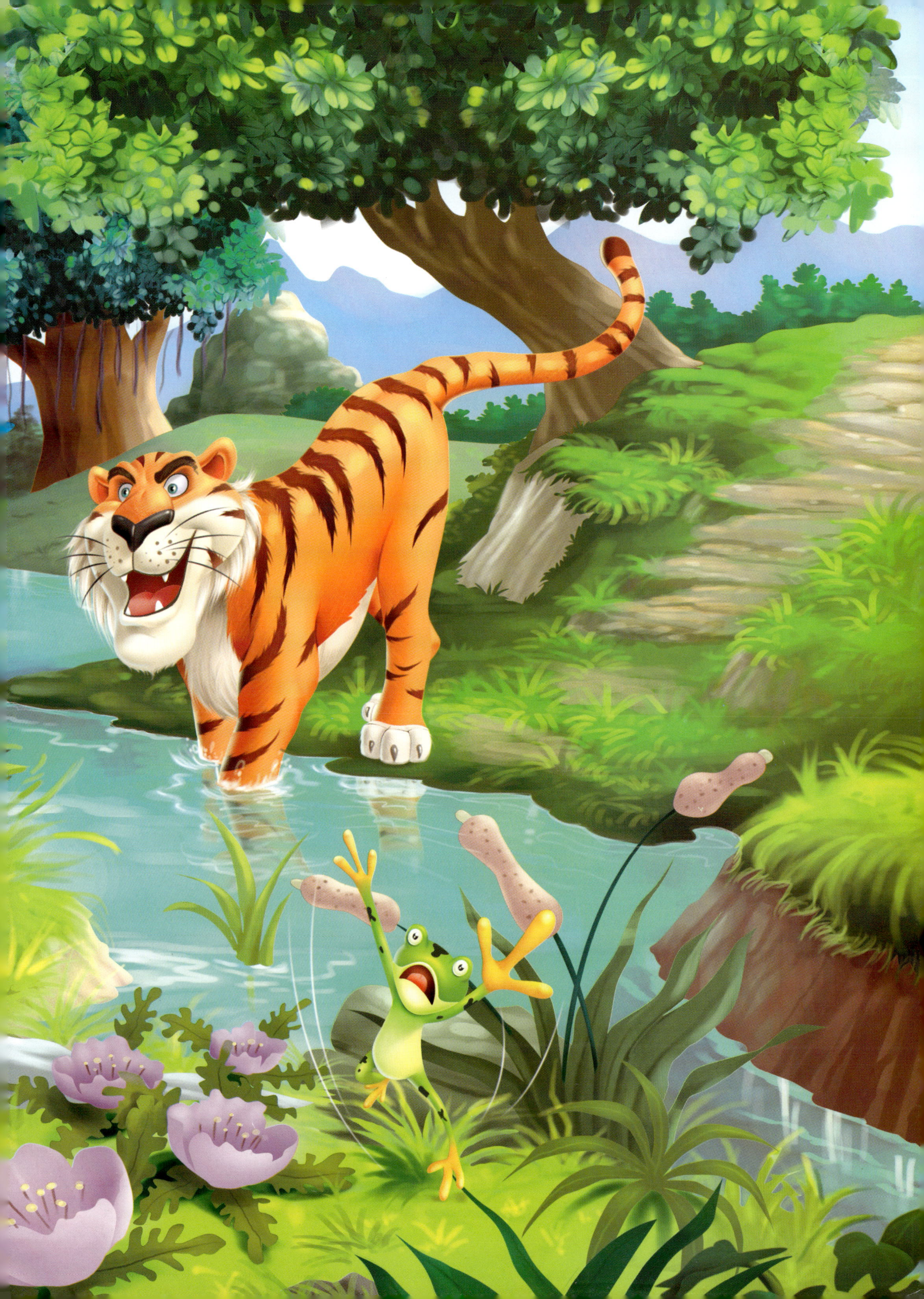

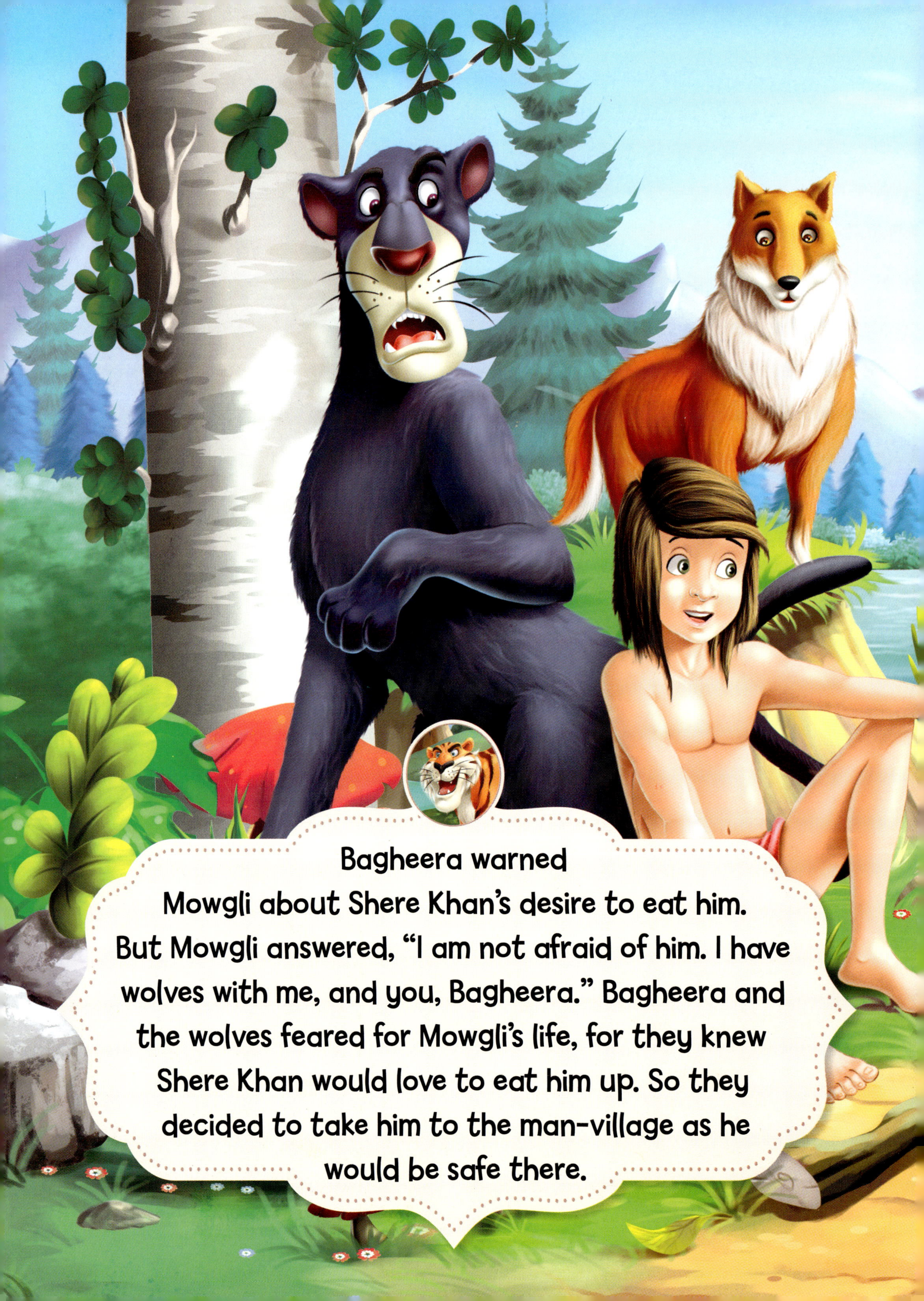

Bagheera warned
Mowgli about Shere Khan's desire to eat him.
But Mowgli answered, "I am not afraid of him. I have wolves with me, and you, Bagheera." Bagheera and the wolves feared for Mowgli's life, for they knew Shere Khan would love to eat him up. So they decided to take him to the man-village as he would be safe there.

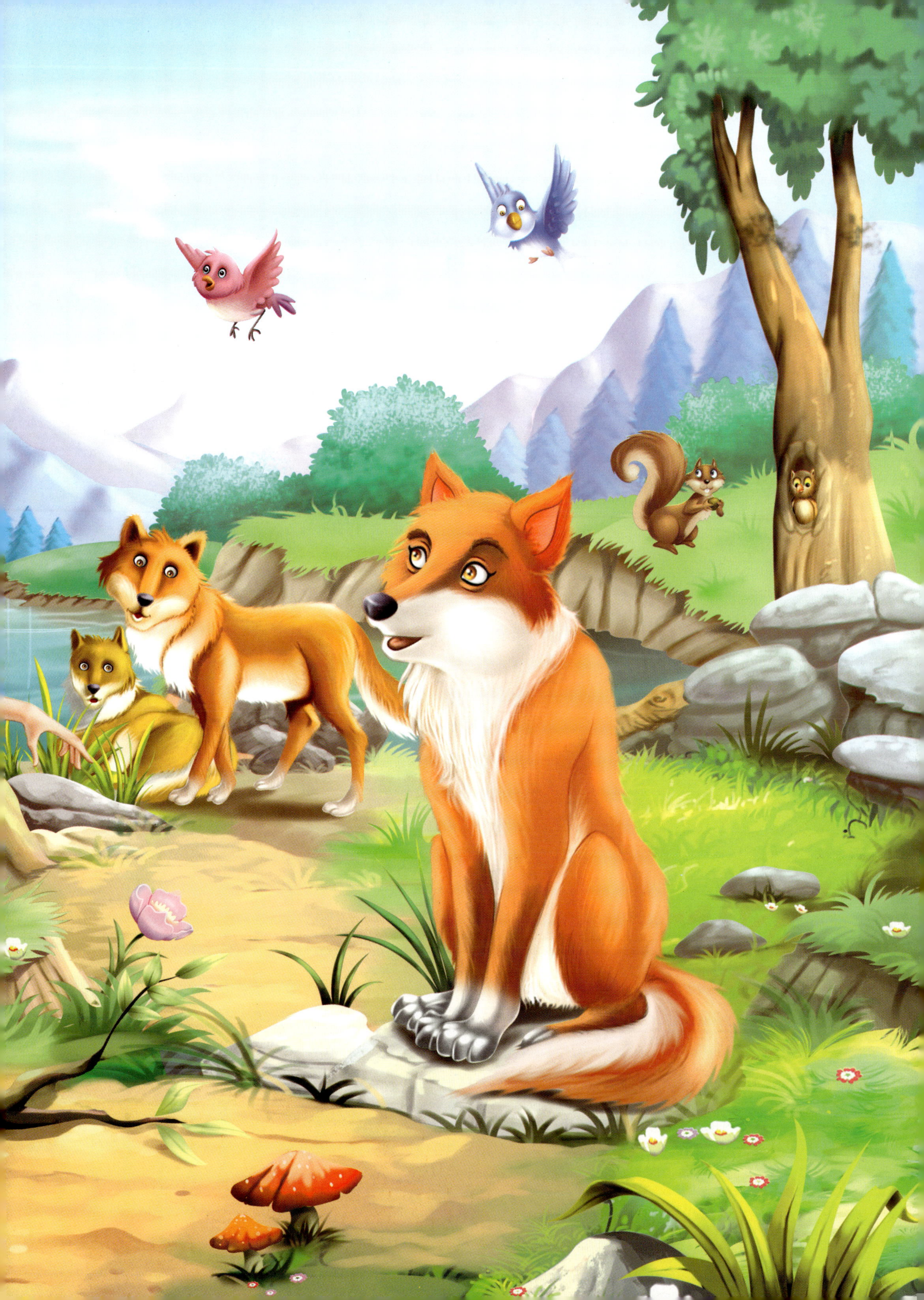

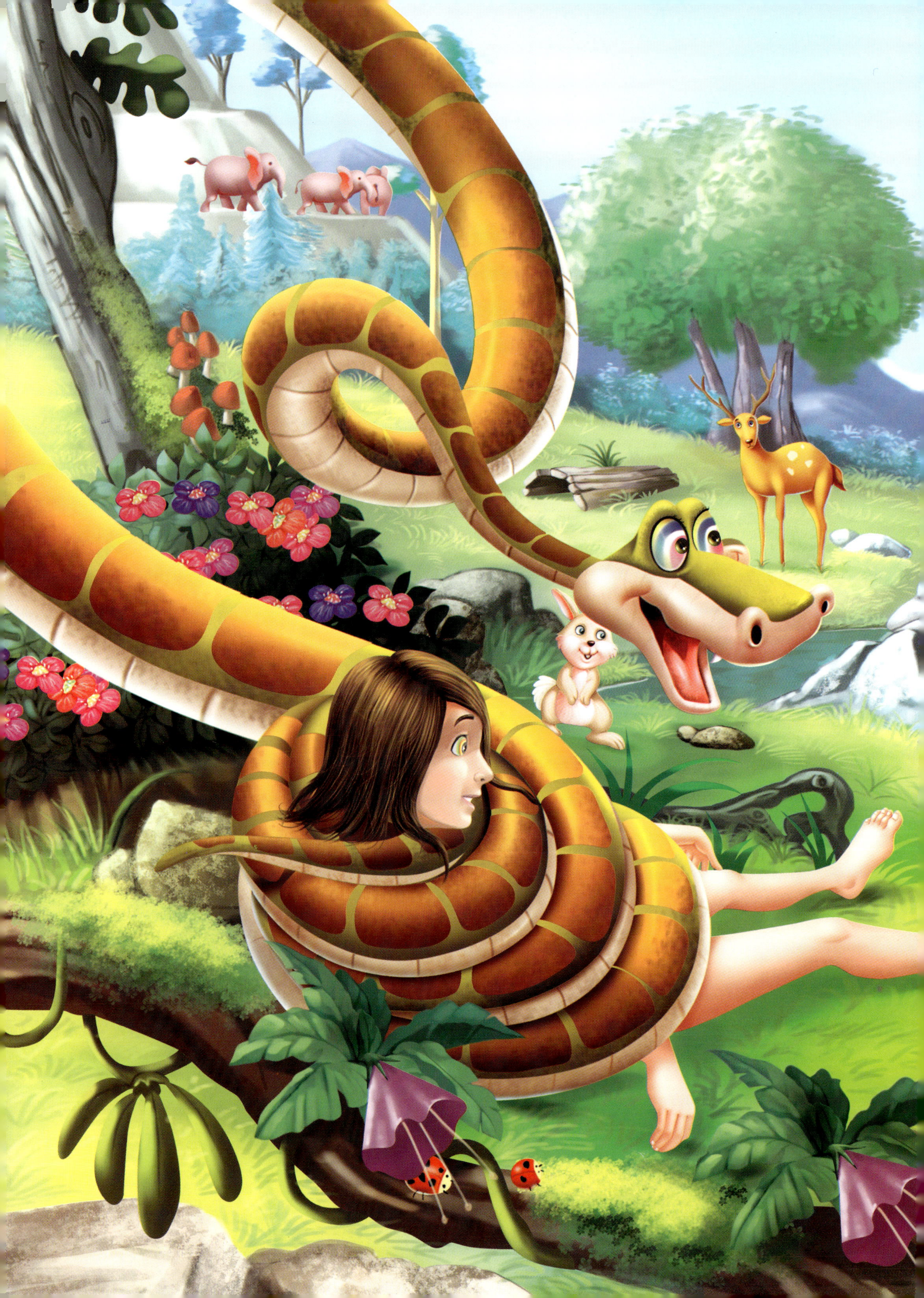

The next morning,
Bagheera and Mowgli set off to the man-village. The village was very far from the jungle. It would take them some days to reach. On their way, they met Kaa, the snake. He trapped Mowgli tightly in his coils and then tried to eat him. Bagheera rushed to rescue Mowgli.

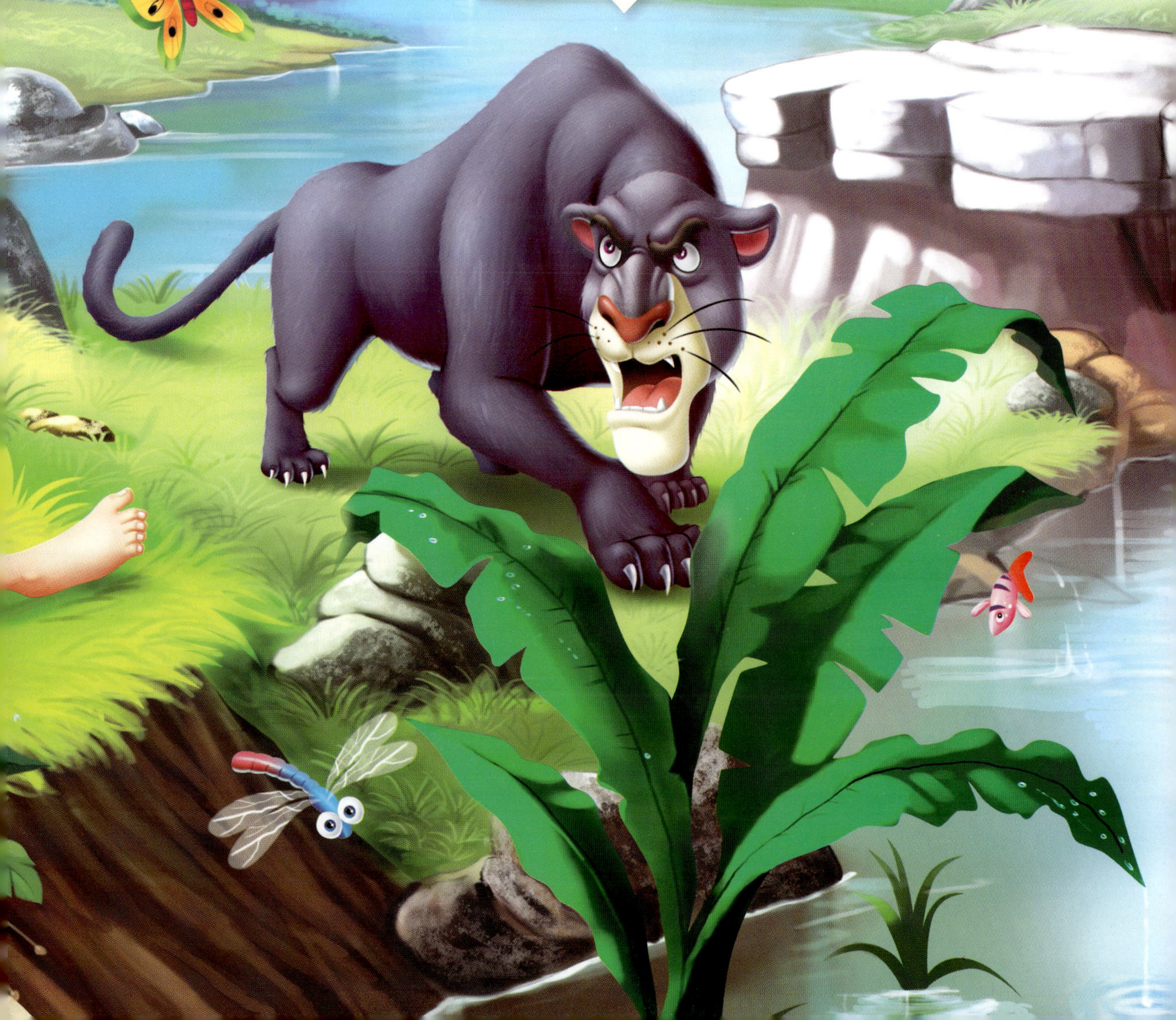

One day, lawless monkeys carried away Mowgli while he was playing with Baloo. He screamed, “Help me, Baloo! Help me, Bagheera!” They promised to set Mowgli free only if he showed them how to light a fire, like a human being. Baloo fought violently by biting the monkeys right and left.

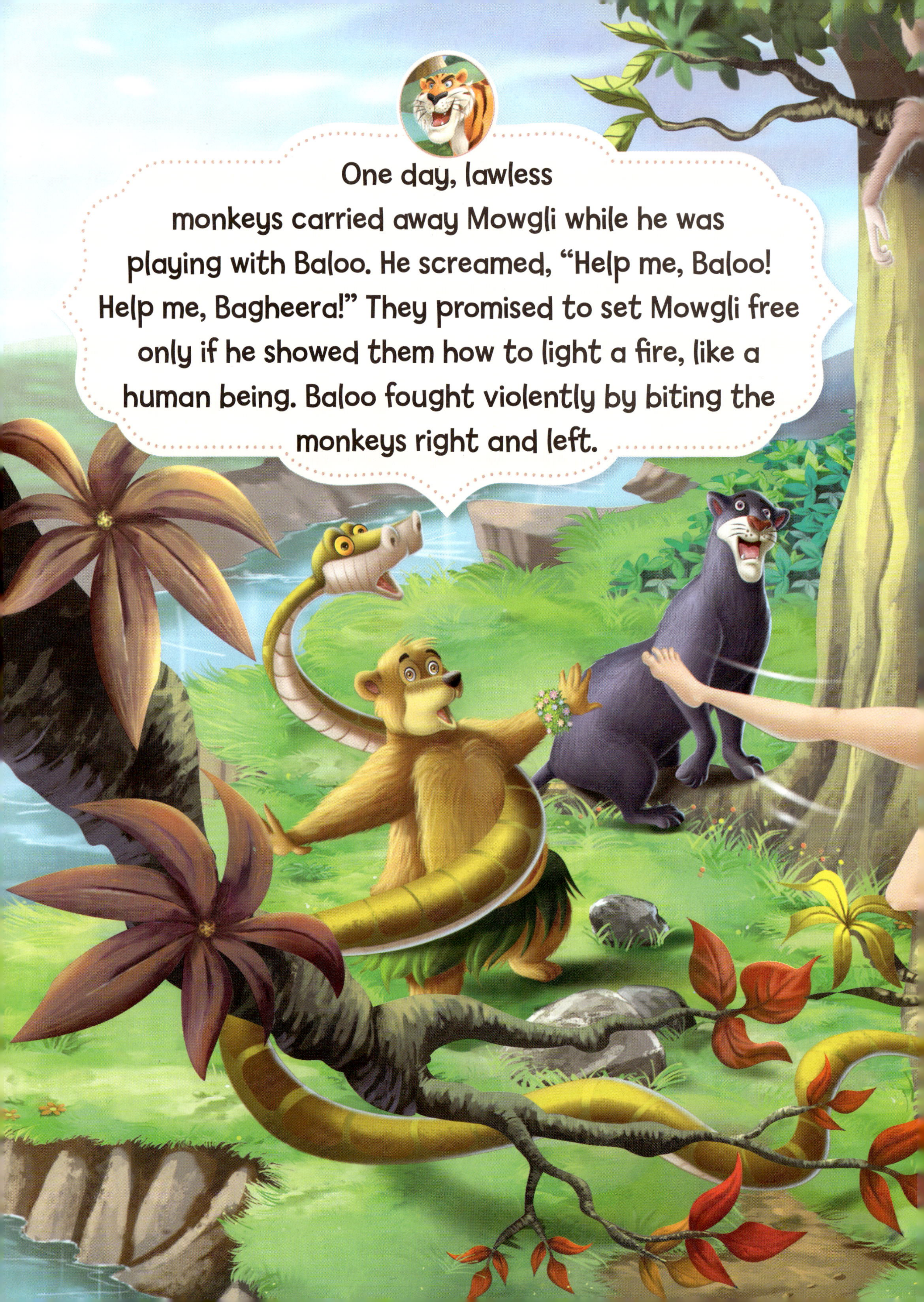

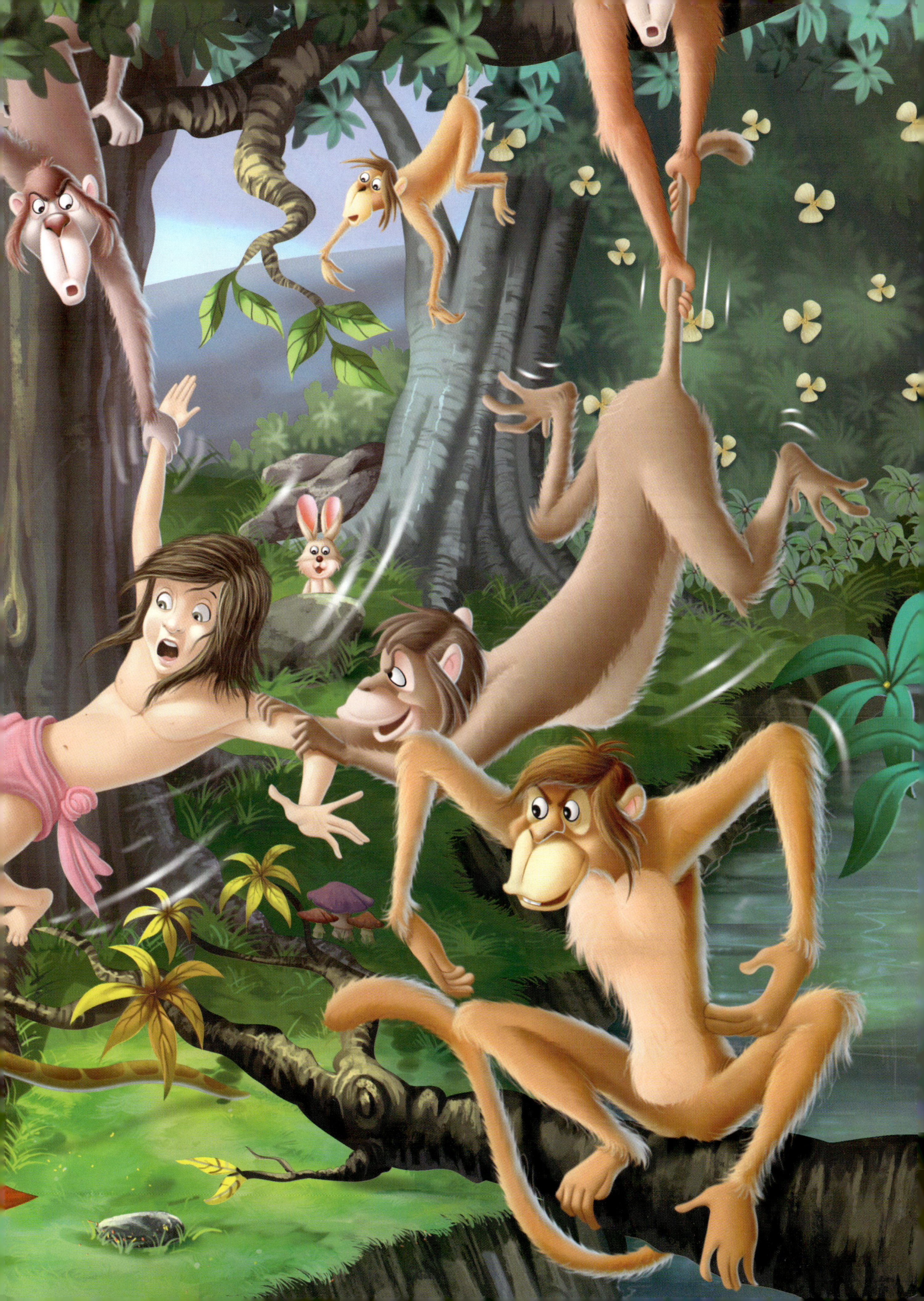

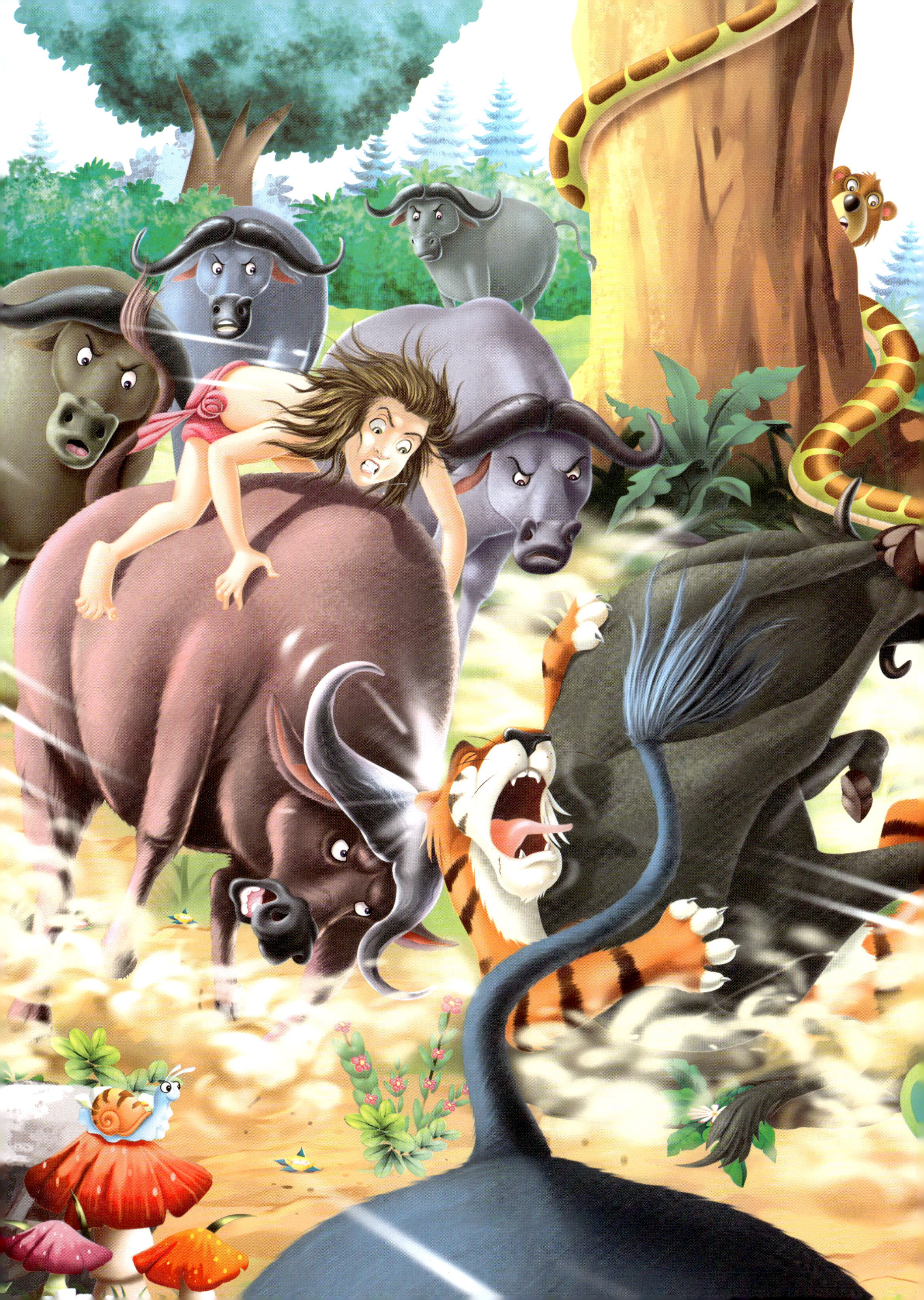

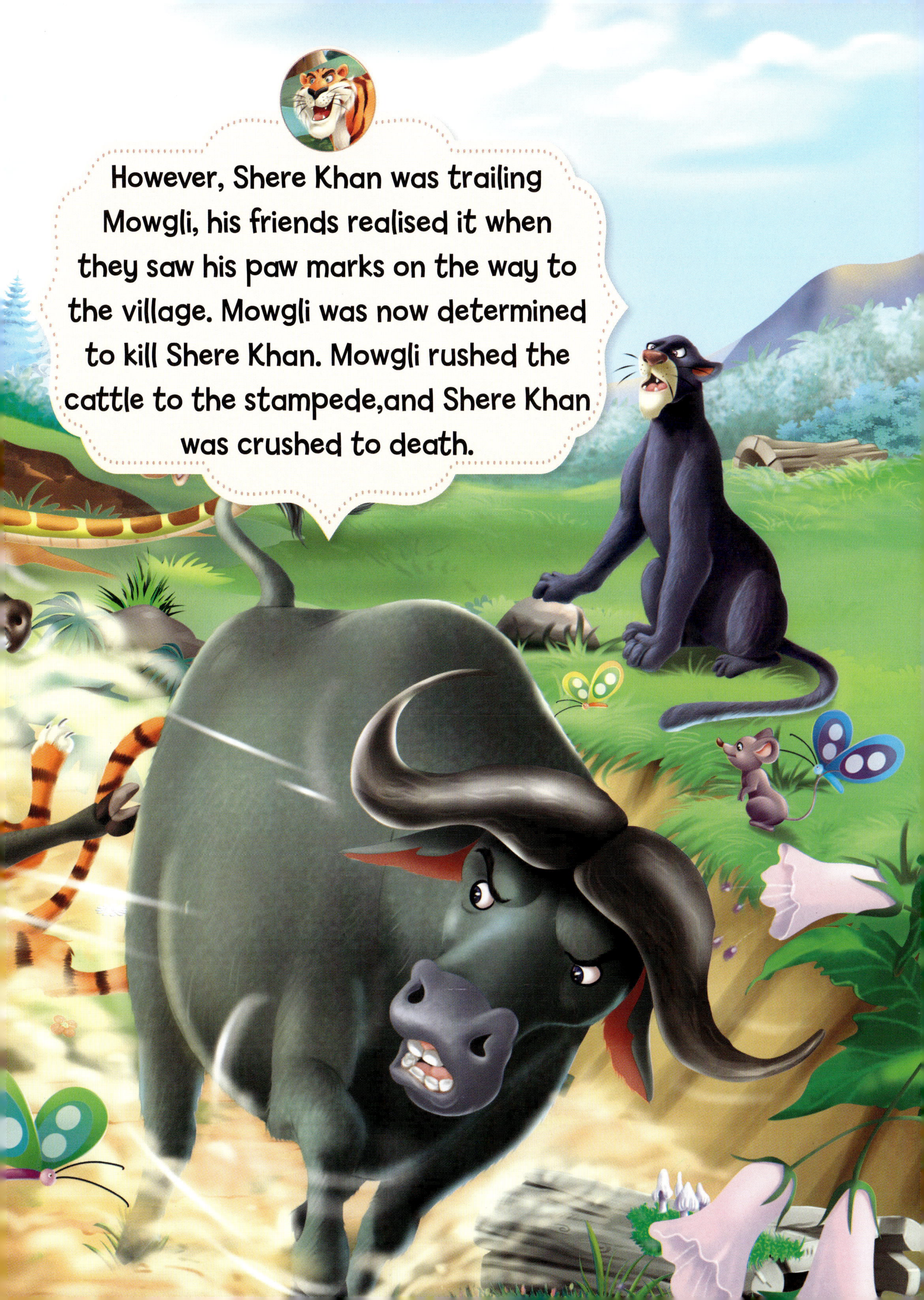
However, Shere Khan was trailing Mowgli, his friends realised it when they saw his paw marks on the way to the village. Mowgli was now determined to kill Shere Khan. Mowgli rushed the cattle to the stampede,and Shere Khan was crushed to death.

Bagheera, Baloo and Kaa took Mowgli to the edge of the man-village. Mowgli was still unwilling to leave his family. Just then, Mowgli saw a young girl who waved and smiled at him. Mowgli was happy to make a new friend and decided to stay in the village.

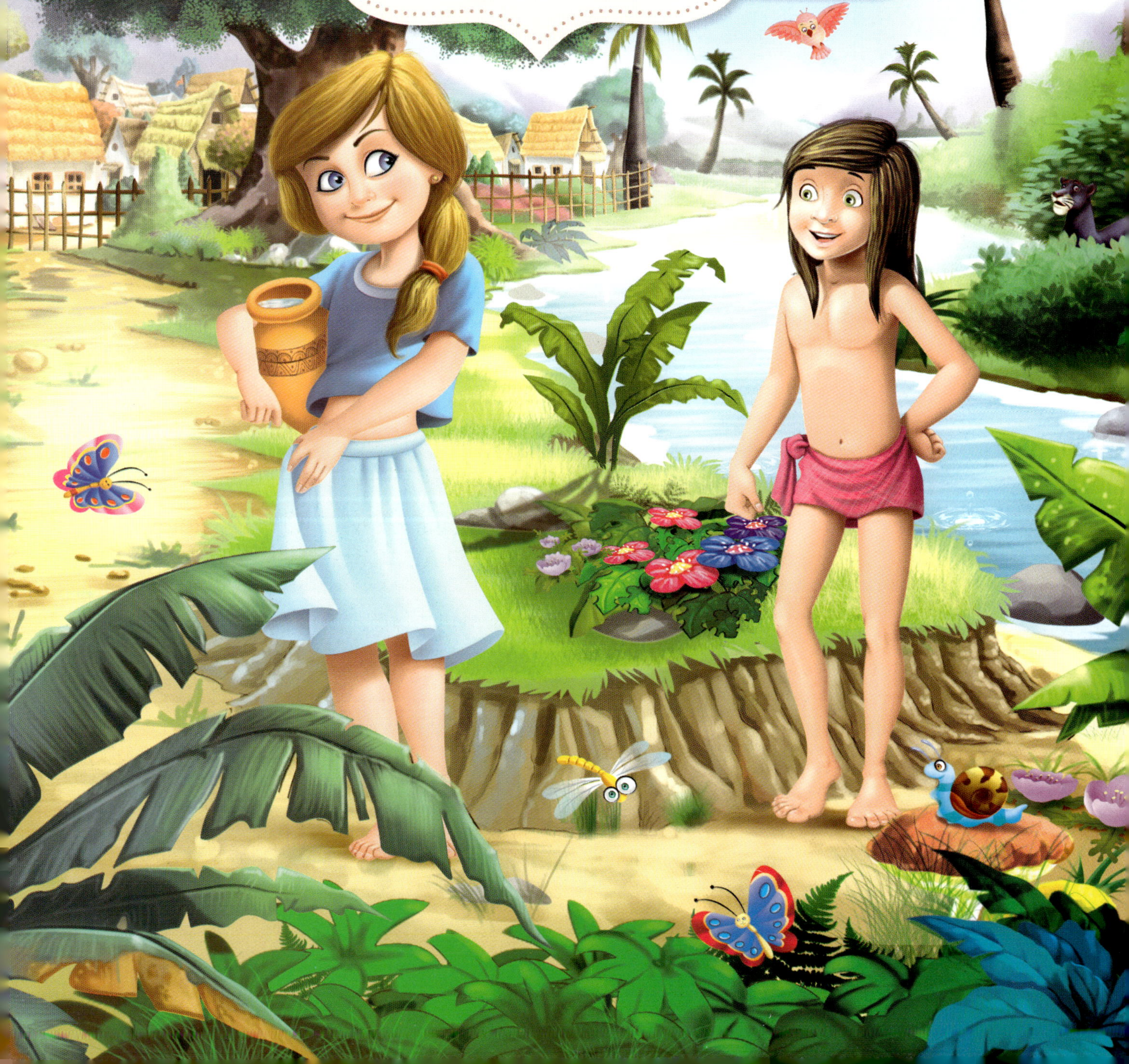